The Survivor Tree
Inspired by a True Story

By Cheryl Somers Aubin
Illustrations by Sheila Harrington

Published in the United States by Callery Press
www.Callerypress.com

ISBN: 978-0-9838334-0-6

Library of Congress Control Number: 2011912393

Aubin, Cheryl Somers

The Survivor Tree: Inspired by a True Story by Cheryl Somers Aubin
www.Thesurvivortree.com

Illustrations and graphic design by Sheila Harrington

First Edition

Summary: A badly injured Callery Pear Tree discovered
under the rubble of the Twin Towers is nursed back to health over a number of years.
She becomes known as the 9/11 Survivor Tree
and is planted at the 9/11 Memorial Plaza in New York City.

[1. Juvenile fiction/ social issues/ emotions and feelings.
2. Juvenile fiction/ historical/ September 11, 2001]

The illustrations in this book were created with pen and ink and watercolor
on Arches 300# cold press watercolor paper.

All profits from the sale of this book go to charity.

Dedication

In memory of those
who perished on 9/11

In gratitude for those
who answered the call for help

In honor of the strength and courage
of all survivors

For more than 20 years, a Callery Pear Tree lived on the World Trade Center Plaza in New York City. On September 11, 2001, the Twin Towers collapsed near her, covering her in debris.

The tree lay under the smoking rubble for a month. Then, one day, some of the workers at the site spotted a few of her green leaves showing through the gray concrete and ash.

Just like our country, the tree was scared, sad, and in shock. But over time, and with great care, she recovered.

This is her story.

The workers carefully uncovered the tree. They saw that most of her limbs had been sheared off and only a few roots remained. Her trunk was scarred and burned. But her green leaves gave them hope that she could be saved.

During the ride on the truck to the nursery where she would be cared for, the tree listened to the sounds of the city soften until all she heard was the rushing wind and the sound of the truck's motor. She felt scared. Everything had changed, and she didn't know what would happen to her. The Callery Pear Tree watched the city grow smaller in the distance and remembered the first time she had ever seen New York City …

On a chilly spring day some twenty years earlier, the tree had been preparing to move to her new home at the World Trade Center Plaza. Although she liked the quiet nursery where she had grown from a seed to a sapling to a tree ten feet tall, she was also very excited about this new adventure.

From her perch on the truck, the Callery Pear Tree couldn't believe all she was seeing and hearing as they approached New York City. Buildings, taller than any tree she had ever seen, reached clear up to the sky. When they entered the city, she was mesmerized by the sounds of traffic, construction, music playing, and many people talking and laughing. Bright lights flashed around her.

The tree tried to hold onto those happy memories and good feelings because she was still feeling scared as she arrived at the nursery. Once she was there, the nursery workers carefully placed her in a hole filled with special fertilizer. As they gently tamped the soft, rich soil around her roots, the tree felt as if she were being wrapped in a warm blanket and started to feel a little safer.

Richie, a City Parks worker, came toward her and looked at her broken branches, the gashes in her trunk, the ash that still covered her. He saw how very hurt she was and hoped she would live. Richie reached out a hand and laid it on her trunk. "I'll do all I can to help you get better. All I can to help you heal."

The Callery Pear Tree sensed a deep sadness in everyone around her, and she felt a great sadness, too. She doubted things would ever be better again.

To make her feel at home in this new place, several workers arrived the next morning with two tall stone blocks and several smaller stone blocks. One by one they quietly placed the stones near her in a memorial shaped like the World Trade Center.

After a winter with little snow, spring arrived in the nursery. The ground softened, the air started to warm, and the nursery began to come alive. Richie visited the tree every day. Some days he carefully pruned her, cutting away the damaged parts of her limbs. She knew that Richie was trying to help her heal, but she felt angry he even had to do this, angry that she was so different now from the beautiful tree she had been. She did not want to go through the hard work of healing.

One day, Richie noticed a collection of twigs in the crook of the tree's limbs. A few days later, he saw a flash of silver descending from the sky, and then a dove appeared with a bit of twine in her beak. She landed near the twigs and added the twine to the nest she was building in the tree. The dove's silver feathers contrasted with the dark bark of the tree. Richie smiled. He felt hopeful for the first time in a very long while.

8

Later that week, Richie spied green buds forming on the tree's branches. His heart filled with joy. He knew at that moment the tree would survive.

The tree basked in the spring sun. She loved hearing the birds singing to each other, feeling the sun encouraging her leaves, shaking off the winter cold. Soon, she was covered in small white blossoms. Once, when Richie arrived to put down fresh fertilizer, she released a shower of petals that floated down and rested on his hair, making him laugh.

One beautiful day, when the sun was warm and the puffy clouds floated lazily across the sky, the Callery Pear Tree remembered a day on the World Trade Center Plaza, a day just like this one …

11

That spring day on the plaza, puffy clouds had floated by in a bright blue sky. Everyone wanted to be outside. The tree's blossoms were in full bloom, making a wide pool of leafy shade.

At lunchtime, a young man carrying a brown paper bag sat down on the end of a bench beneath the tree's canopy. He pulled out a sandwich, cracked open a paperback book, and lost himself reading as he ate his lunch.

A little while later, a young woman carrying a bagel and a
notebook arrived and sat on the other end of the bench. She pulled a
cassette player out of her purse and put on her headphones. Listening
to music, she looked off in the distance, pausing occasionally to take a
bite of her bagel or write in her notebook.

Once their lunch hours ended, the two stood up to leave and nearly collided
as they crossed paths. They smiled and parted with a shy, "Hello."

During that spring, the tree had witnessed a gentle and slow courtship. As the days passed, the young man and woman began sitting a bit closer to each other. Then, one day, he glanced over at her and put down his book. The young woman smiled and took off her headphones. They began to talk.

Throughout the spring of 2001, the couple came together at lunchtime in the tree's shade. They held hands and talked, sharing their lunches and their dreams for the future. Sometimes she would laugh, showing a beautiful smile. He would smile, too, happy that he had made her laugh.

A few more years passed at the nursery, and the tree continued healing and getting stronger every day. Another summer arrived.

Summertime at the nursery was hot, but not as hot as it had been at the Plaza. The tree's fruit had come in—small, round, red berries that looked more like crab apples than pears. The birds came in the early morning to eat them, and the bees buzzed around her leafy tips in slow circles, riding the breeze that cooled the tree every once in a while.

There were still times when she felt hopeless. The tree worried that, even though she was getting better, things would never be the same.

Richie came by every morning to check on her and water her. Her leaves wilted a bit in the heat, and she loved getting watered, loved the way the water soaked into the ground so she could catch it with her roots and drink it in.

One day, as the Callery Pear Tree listened to the sound of the water from the hose splashing on the ground, she remembered the World Trade Center Plaza and the musical sound of the fountain. It was a summer day, a day just like this one …

The summers in New York City had been very, very hot.
Her leaves often wilted and drooped. The humid air would sap all the energy out of everyone—including the tree. But she had loved watching the sun reflecting off the windows of the tall buildings, creating bright flashes of light that danced across the Plaza, and she had loved the fountain.

A huge brass ball had anchored the middle of the fountain's large circle. The water flowed gently outward and then over the sides, making a sound like a gentle brook.

Sometimes the water in the fountain was turned on full force, and small spires of water would shoot up in the air a foot or two, then come crashing back down like a waterfall. Children would lean over and splash their hands in the water, and sometimes adults did, too.

The tree had been most happy in the early summer mornings, just as the sun was lighting the sky. The air was clear, and it seemed as if the fountain were playing just for her.

Seasons came and went, and a few more years passed at the nursery. The tree was much stronger and taller now. Another autumn arrived.

She welcomed the cooler air, the winds that rose softly, then blew strong, then softly again. Autumn was one of her favorite seasons. Each year at this time, her leaves slowly changed from green to beautiful burgundy, bright red, and soft orange.

On a cool, crisp day with clear skies, a New York City firefighter came to visit the tree in the nursery. He approached her slowly, then removed his hat and stood in front of her with his head bowed, traces of tears on his face. He whispered to her, "I know it's been hard for you. It's been hard on all of us, but I want to thank you so much for making it, for surviving."

She saw the strength she'd given him and realized that she mattered.

With great concentration, she was able to release a single leaf exactly so it fell on his shoulder, tapping him ever so lightly. He looked up at the beautiful colors of her leaves and faintly smiled.

Later, as night fell and the evening breeze picked up, she watched her colorful leaves swirling and dancing in the air as they took flight on the autumn breeze.

The Callery Pear Tree then remembered one autumn night on the Plaza and the colorful clothes people wore when they came to listen to salsa music and dance, swirling round and round …

It had been a very exciting night on the Plaza. People from
all over New York City arrived, dressed up in bright colors, to hear the
salsa music and dance under the stars. The music was electrifying.
By the end of the night, the entire plaza was filled with dancers
laughing and singing.

When the wind picked up, the tree swayed and imagined she was
dancing to the music, too.

The last winter the tree would spend at the nursery finally arrived. She was about 30 feet tall. Strong and healthy. The scars on her trunk were less visible, but she knew they were there, knew all she had gone through to have come this far.

It had only snowed a few days by then, leaving small traces of snow on the ground around her. On one of those days, she watched the snow fall quietly in the nursery. She loved to watch it fall, watch every snowflake, marvel at the beauty of nature and the sky that changed from blue to light gray.

When the small, light flakes were falling, flakes that disappeared before they landed, the Callery Pear Tree remembered a day on the World Trade Center Plaza when people were skating on an ice rink. She remembered a day just like this one …

Even though the skating rink had been on the Plaza for just a few years, it was one of the tree's favorite winter memories. She had loved watching the skaters on the rink, the people from all over the city who would come there. Sometimes they would take a break and sit on her bench, drinking coffee and watching the other skaters.

The skaters glided by at their own pace, faces flushed from the cold, smiling and calling to each other. Some of the more experienced skaters would gather in the middle of the rink to practice turns and jumps.

One day, a six-year-old boy in a red hat tried to learn how to skate. Another day, a family of six all held hands and skated together, the youngest child in the middle.

Later, one man, showing off for his girlfriend, skated too fast and landed right on his backside. They both started laughing, and then she fell down, too.

During the tree's last week at the nursery, on a clear and cold day in mid-December, Richie came to see her.

"Some workers will be coming for you tomorrow to take you back to the World Trade Center to live at the 9/11 Memorial Plaza," Richie told her. "You mean so much to so many people, and everyone is excited to see you going back home."

She wondered what it would be like to return to the city. She felt excited and curious.

Richie smiled at her, but his eyes were brimming with tears. "We are all so proud of you," he whispered to her as he put a hand on her trunk. He would miss her very much. The tree would miss Richie, too. She released one of her few remaining burgundy leaves. It floated gently down and tapped him right on his nose. He looked down at the leaf, picked it up and put it in his pocket. This leaf he would keep for himself.

The next day, the workers from the nursery dug a large hole around her. It tickled the Callery Pear Tree's roots a little. The men and women, many of whom had also helped care for her all these years, wrapped her root ball in burlap and helped guide her onto the truck. They all said goodbye.

When the Callery Pear Tree approached New York City again, she saw short and tall buildings and lights streaming into the sky. She heard the familiar sounds of traffic and honking horns. She loved the cold, invigorating wind whipping through her branches. As she was planted in the ground, she saw the construction of the memorial still taking place all around her. This area looked so very different to her, but it still felt like home.

In a ceremony to celebrate her return, the mayor gave a speech. Other officials and several people who survived the collapse of the buildings on September 11, 2001, were also there. They all called her the 9/11 Survivor Tree. She felt humbled and honored and proud.

By springtime, the tree's branches were once again full of blossoms.

One day, the tree spotted a man and a woman in the distance holding hands with a small girl between them. They were heading right toward the tree.

As they came closer, the Callery Pear Tree could suddenly make out familiar faces. It was the couple who had met and courted on her bench all those years ago.

The father lifted his daughter up onto his shoulders. "This is the tree where Mommy and I met," he told her. The three of them gazed up at the tree while the mother and father told the story of their courtship. "This is a very special tree," the mother said.

The little girl reached out her hand, and the tree brushed her soft petals against the girl's cheek. She laughed. "Special tree," she said.

The spring sun was growing brighter in the sky, and the wind picked up, ruffling the tree's leaves. The family turned to leave.

The tree watched them walk away. Before they went too far, the little girl looked back and waved goodbye to the tree.

The tree dug her roots in a bit deeper and stretched her limbs up to the sky.

She had survived. The Callery Pear Tree was truly home.

Acknowledgments

I wish to thank Richie Cabo, for his incredible kindness toward me and for his generosity in allowing me to tell the story of his relationship with the 9/11 Survivor Tree. It has been my honor to come to know this caring man. I extend my thanks to all the City Parks workers who also helped care for the tree.

I am so very grateful to Mary Owen, LCSW, whose expertise and gentle guidance helped me to understand about trauma, healing, and recovery.

Kathy Webster, Debra Bruno, Ed Perlman, and Patty Donahue all read the manuscript and offered excellent advice.

For sharing memories of their lives working and living near the World Trade Center, I thank Marilyn Puder-York and Lorrie Stapleton.

A special thanks to Debbie Levy, the members of my Writer Moms Group, Lois Baron, Maureen McDowell Weschler, Helen Johnsen, and Kelly Peterson for their help on the book and their incredible support of me. Thank you, too, to Cristian Torres and Bea and Tim Webster.

I am indebted to Sheila Harrington, who contributed to this book not only with helpful suggestions on the manuscript but also with her beautiful watercolors that capture the true essence of the story.

My parents, Don and Nancy Somers, have always encouraged my creativity and believed in this book from the first moment I mentioned it to them.

And, with love and gratitude, I thank my husband, Steve, for reading the manuscript and reviewing it with me over and over and over again, for the wonderful advice he gave me, and for telling me almost daily, "You can do this!" I thank our son, Charles, for being such a great kid and for his expertise in all things computer-related. Their unwavering support and understanding of me carried me through the many months of writing this book.

—*Cheryl Somers Aubin*

About the Author

Cheryl Somers Aubin has been writing and publishing for over twenty years, and her work has appeared in *The Washington Post*, *Boston Globe*, *Foundation Magazine*, and other newspapers, magazines, and on-line journals. She has a Master of Arts degree in Writing from Johns Hopkins University. Cheryl teaches memoir writing and creative writing that incorporates artwork. She has been an instructor at Johns Hopkins University and a featured speaker at personal history writing symposia, writing conferences and workshops.

Cheryl authored two essays in the book *From the Heart: A Collection of Stories and Poems from the Front Lines of Parenting*. Her non-fiction and fiction work can be seen on her website: www.cherylaubin.com. This is her first book.

About the Artist

Sheila Harrington is a painter, illustrator, and graphic designer whose work has ranged from portraiture to print design to museum exhibition graphics. She is a partner with her artist/designer husband, James Symons, in the Washington, DC art and design firm Studio Five. Her work can be seen on its website, www.studio5dc.com.

She also maintains an art blog, Each Day is a Celebration, www.sheilaharrington.org/eachday.

CPSIA information can be obtained
at www.ICGtesting.com
Printed in the USA
LVIC04n1516190914
404928LV00004B/8

* 9 7 8 0 9 8 3 8 3 3 4 0 6 *